FALLING IN LOVE

ALL OVER AGAIN

The Sullivans

Babymoon Novella

Lori and Grayson

Bella Andre

FALLING IN LOVE ALL OVER AGAIN
The Sullivans
Babymoon Novella
Lori and Grayson
© 2018 Bella Andre

Sign up for Bella's New Release Newsletter
www.BellaAndre.com/newsletter
bella@bellaandre.com
www.BellaAndre.com
Bella on Twitter: @bellaandre
Bella on Facebook: facebook.com/bellaandrefans

Lori "Naughty" Sullivan has always been a force of nature—and marriage to Grayson Tyler, her sexy cowboy, hasn't mellowed her out one bit. She's still dancing in stilettos, laughing too loud, and lovingly plotting new ways to drive her husband crazy. It's almost time for their most exciting adventure yet, and Lori can't wait for the next phase of their lives to begin—as parents. Especially when she's certain that Grayson is going to be the best father ever. But has he truly made peace with his tragic past? Or will it come back to haunt him just when their future together should have never looked brighter?

A note from Bella

The question I'm asked most often is: *Do you have a favorite Sullivan?*

Honestly, I don't. Mostly because I fall head over heels in love with every single Sullivan while I'm writing his or her story.

But if I *had* to choose a favorite Sullivan, Lori would certainly be in the running for a spot at the top of the list.

I absolutely adored writing her love story in *Always On My Mind*. Years later, I'm thrilled to have the chance to check back in with Lori and Grayson in *Falling In Love All Over Again* as they embark on the next exciting stage of their lives.

I hope you enjoy reading this novella as much I did writing it!

If this is your first time reading about the Sullivans, you can easily read each book as a stand-alone—and there is a Sullivan family tree available on my website (www.bellaandre.com/sullivan-family-tree) so you can see how the books are connected!

Happy reading,
Bella Andre

P.S. Many more Sullivan love stories are coming soon! Please be sure to sign up for my newsletter (bellaandre.com/newsletter) so that you don't miss out on any new book announcements.

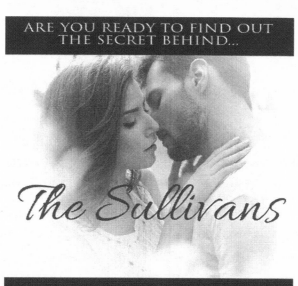

CHAPTER ONE

Lori Sullivan-Tyler wasn't looking for trouble.

Actually, that wasn't true. She was trouble in high heels—a master at causing the maximum amount of havoc in the minimum amount of time. Even at eight months pregnant, as she and her husband, Grayson, walked up the path to her mother's front door for their baby shower, she was itching to be naughty.

Naughty was her nickname, after all.

When she was a little girl, her brother, Chase, had nicknamed Lori *Naughty* and her twin sister, Sophie, *Nice*. The names fit them perfectly...at least until you dived beneath the surface.

Sophie was a textbook librarian—quiet, neat as a pin, and soft-spoken. But she was a tiger underneath.

As for Lori? Well, she certainly was naughty. But she had plenty of *nice* in her too.

Especially when it came to her husband.

Mmmm, Grayson.

Everything about him made her smile—and heat up all over. He could be grumpy, bossy, domineering...and also crazy, wicked hot. There were few things she loved more than her husband growling at her in bed, while his big, strong hands touched her in *all* the right places.

They were halfway up the front walk when she stumbled over a crack. Of course Grayson was right there when she needed him, sliding his arm around her waist to steady her and the baby.

"Are you okay?"

She smiled up into his beautiful brown eyes, so full of concern. It never ceased to amaze her that he was hers—that a man so honorable, so trustworthy, so caring and strong loved her as much as she loved him. "I'm perfect."

Her response erased the worried look on his face. He bent to kiss her at the same moment that she went onto her tippy-toes to press her lips to his. She would have been happy to keep kissing him forever had her mother not opened the front door a few breathless kisses later.

"Lori, Grayson! I'm so happy to see you both."

Mary Sullivan's hugs were legendary for their warmth and comfort. Her smile was huge as she kissed them each on the cheek, then ushered them inside.

Mary had raised eight children single-handedly after Lori's dad passed away unexpectedly at forty-two. Thinking back on her behavior as a teenager, Lori didn't know how her mother hadn't chucked her out of the house on those days when she'd been mouthing off and acting like a know-it-all jerk. More than a decade later, Lori marveled at just how amazing her mom was. Putting a hand over her baby bump, she couldn't wait to be as good a mother to her own daughter.

From the delicious-looking spread set out across every flat surface, Lori figured her mother must have been cooking and baking for days. Lori and Grayson had offered to hire catering and servers for the party, but Mary had insisted that she was more than happy to take care of the food and drinks, just as she always did.

No question about it, Lori's mom knew better than anyone how to feed a huge family. Not only would Lori's siblings and their fiancés and wives and children all be here today, but plenty of her cousins had also decided the baby shower was the perfect opportunity to take a California vacation. Though there had already been several Sullivan weddings, birthdays, and her Uncle William's gallery unveiling in Alexandria Bay, New York, this year, Lori couldn't wait to see everyone again.

The house and backyard were beautifully decorated, the party setting both elegant and festive with pink, magenta, and purple accents. Knowing mass chaos would descend once the kids arrived and started running around, Lori pulled out her phone to take some pictures while everything was still pristine and perfect.

"You're looking great, honey," Mary said to Lori. "How are you feeling?"

"I feel incredible." Lori wasn't just saying it to keep her mother from worrying. She had buckets of energy. Especially when it came to seducing her husband. For the past handful of months, her libido had been brimming over. "My biggest problem is how impatient I am to meet the baby. I wish we didn't have to wait three and a half more weeks. Maybe even up to five weeks, if I go past my due date like you did when you had Marcus."

"In my experience," her mother replied as she stroked Lori's hair just as she always had, "babies come exactly when they're supposed to. Although I have a feeling it won't be too long until this little one makes an appearance." Mary's eyes were warm as she turned to Grayson. "And how are *you* feeling?"

"As long as Lori feels good, I'm good."

He drew Lori to him, and she snuggled against his broad chest. Grayson had never been a man of many words. He'd always spoken more with actions, with a touch and a smile.

"He's been the best husband ever. Lots of foot rubs, grilling us feasts for dinner, and he's been feeding the chickens so I can take more time with the pigs.

Which is the only place I've had to draw the line—they seem so sad when I don't personally muck out their stalls and feed them."

"You agreed that you'd stop going into the pigpen if your balance started to go." A frown line appeared between his brows.

"My balance is great. In fact, I could still do a pirouette on a tightrope." She moved into the center of the kitchen to demonstrate and was halfway through her spin when Summer's poodle darted past and knocked into her. Mary had been watching the dog this past week while Lori's brother Gabe, his wife, Megan, and their children, Summer and Logan, were on vacation.

Grayson caught Lori before she could so much as stumble. "My hero," Lori said, putting her hand on his cheek.

Though she was obviously unharmed, his frown had gone even deeper. And she knew why—her husband was innately protective, and as soon as they'd found out that she was pregnant, his need to keep her safe had gone into overdrive.

Though fiercely independent, Lori loved her husband for exactly who he was. Lord knew he could be difficult sometimes—an immovable boulder of a man, in fact. Had she been a woman who had trouble speaking up for herself, their relationship would surely never have worked.

Fortunately, she had no problem whatsoever pushing back if she ever felt constrained or misunderstood. Granted, sometimes that pushback took the form of sassy comments or stormy behavior. At the same time, Lori's mother had raised her well, teaching her not only to apologize when she was wrong, but also to ask for forgiveness when she took things a step—or a dozen steps—too far.

Good thing Lori knew exactly how to put her husband at ease. Their guests wouldn't be arriving for at least fifteen minutes. It wasn't a ton of time to put Operation Relax Grayson into action, but she was positive that the time she had to take his mind off his worries would definitely be worth it.

Before she could whisk him out of the kitchen, however, he asked her mother, "What can we help you with, Mary?"

Her mother waved away his offer. "You know me—I had everything ready by seven o'clock this morning. Why don't the two of you get a drink and relax for a bit before everyone arrives?"

"Thanks, Mom, will do," Lori said. "First, though, there's something I need to show Grayson in my old bedroom."

"Take as much time as you need together before you come out to greet the masses." As Mary picked up

two bottles of white wine and headed into the backyard to chill them in a bucket of ice, Lori wondered if
her mother had guessed her plan. Though her mom
obviously wasn't a virgin—not with eight kids—the
thought of her having sexy-times with her father still
made Lori blush.

"Are you sure there isn't something we could help
your mother with?" Grayson looked out the window to
the backyard, where Mary was tying down a corner of
a tablecloth that had blown free in the breeze.

"My mom could throw a brilliant party for one
hundred people with five minutes' notice and both
hands tied behind her back—and she truly does like
taking care of the details herself. Besides, before the
party starts, you *really* need to see what's in my old
bedroom."

Grayson looked adorably suspicious. "What could
you possibly have to show me that you haven't shown
me before?"

"You'll see." She took his hand and led him
through the dining and living rooms, toward the
bedrooms.

Apart from a remodeled kitchen and bathrooms,
and some new upholstery on the couch, the house was
the same as it had been when Lori and her siblings
were growing up. As the youngest of the group
alongside her twin, Lori had only ever known a home

that was loud and crazy and full of love. *LoudCrazyLove* was her default setting, she thought with a grin. Whereas Grayson had grown up as the only child in a perfectly pristine New York City brownstone, where *polite and well-mannered* was the order of the day.

Were it not for a twist of fate, Lori and Grayson might never have met. Several years ago, when she had learned that her then boyfriend was a lying, cheating scum, she had fled Chicago, where she had been choreographing a show, and ended up in Pescadero, a wild and remote farm town on the Northern California coast. She'd stopped in at the local general store for a sandwich and found a FARMHAND NEEDED sign. Though she made her living as a dancer and choreographer, she was so hell-bent on leaving her past behind that she hadn't thought twice before applying for the job. After all, what could be more different and strange and divergent from the life she'd always lived than working on a thousand-acre farm? There, she had planned to kick all men to the curb forever.

But she hadn't counted on meeting her tall, gorgeous, reserved, and extremely loving cowboy.

Though she and Grayson had been oil and water at first—every word out of his mouth had been a challenge she couldn't back away from—he was the best thing that had ever happened to her. Not to mention the most shockingly sexy. Two hundred pounds of tanned muscle, his square jaw dusted with dark stubble—every time she looked into his eyes, butterflies flew inside her belly.

It wasn't long before she'd learned about his tragic past and the grief and guilt that he carried inside himself. She had been determined to help him find the joy in life again the only way she knew how—with laughter, fun, adventure, and love.

Plus lots and lots of hot, sticky, sweaty, breath-stealing sex, of course.

She had been so happy when he'd finally started to climb out of the darkness. What she hadn't realized was that she would rise up too, when his love and support had helped her rediscover her love of dancing.

As soon as they were inside her old bedroom, Lori reached around Grayson to lock the door, then immediately started unbuckling his belt.

He gave her one of his dark looks as he covered her hands with his much bigger ones, his callused skin giving her the best kind of shivers. His voice was gruff as he said, "You're not planning what I think you're planning, are you?"

She laughed. How could she not when he was everything she'd ever dreamed of, and then some? "How about you tell me what you think I'm planning—or better yet, *show* me—and then I'll tell you if you're right."

Though she could tell that he wanted nothing more than to do just that, he reminded her, "Your uncles, aunts, sister, cousins—and brothers who will surely want to beat me to a pulp if they suspect I'm so much as looking at you sideways—will be arriving any minute. And your mother is just down the hall."

"First of all, my mom has eight kids. So I'm pretty sure she was down for plenty of hijinks when my dad was still around. And my brothers won't want to beat you up. They think you're great."

"Only when they can fool themselves into believing that I've left you as pure as the driven snow."

She looked down at her very rounded stomach, showcased by the soft red fabric of her dress. "It's pretty clear that horse is out of the barn."

"You'd be surprised at how many lies a guy can tell himself. Especially when it comes to wanting to take care of someone he loves."

She had to kiss him then, this wonderful man who would protect her with his dying breath. "I'll be quiet." She could barely get out such a fib. Certainly couldn't keep her eyes from twinkling as she spoke.

"You're *never* quiet."

"You have only yourself to blame for that." She pressed her breasts—which had increased by two cup sizes during her pregnancy, much to Grayson's delight—against his chest. "If you weren't such an incredible lover, I would be able to stay quiet as a mouse."

At last, he gave in and pulled her closer, putting his hands on her hips and groaning into her hair. "You drive me crazy."

She wound her arms around his neck. "I love you too."

CHAPTER TWO

Grayson Tyler couldn't get enough of his wife as his mouth claimed hers, and his hands roamed her luscious curves. From the first moment he'd set eyes on her, he'd been utterly spellbound, growing more and more enthralled every day they were together.

After he'd moved far outside of the city to Pescadero on the self-imposed isolation of a thousand acres of rolling farmland, and before Lori had come into his life, he had shut himself off from the world. He'd blamed himself for not recognizing his late wife's problem with alcohol until it was too late—and for not being able to rewind time and undo the car accident that had taken her life. He had planned on being alone forever...until the day a car he didn't recognize had driven up his long gravel driveway, swerved to avoid a chicken, and crashed into a fencepost.

When Lori emerged from the car, Grayson had been beyond stunned. Never in his life had he seen such a beautiful woman. Nor had he expected her to try to catch the runaway chicken while wearing sequins and spike heels.

He had been rude—worse than that, he had been downright mean—as he'd tried to send her on her way. But she had been irritatingly stubborn and refused to leave.

The farther away he'd tried to push her, the closer she'd come.

Thank God.

Lori Sullivan had blown into his life without the slightest hint of warning. Her beauty had aroused him, her big mouth had irritated him—but it was her laughter that had changed everything for him.

She was not only the person he loved most in the world, she was also a partner who stood her ground like no other. Utterly determined, she was the most fun, loving person on the planet.

All along, he had thought he wanted a quiet, simple life. He grinned as he thought how boring that would be compared to the joyful roller-coaster ride Lori had taken him on from the very first day.

Feeling his grin against her lips, she drew back. "You're not thinking about something from the farm, are you? Like how silly the pigs were being this morning before we left?"

Loving to tease her, he replied, "You know how much I appreciate farm animals and their antics."

"I'll show you antics." Laughter and arousal lit her

eyes as she stepped back and did a little shimmy.

A scrap of red lace fell to her feet, and his heart rate went up at least fifty beats per minute. They'd made love that morning, and the night before, for that matter, but it wasn't enough.

He could *never* get enough of his wife.

"With everyone showing up soon," she said, "I wasn't actually planning on getting naked. But what the heck, let's walk on the wild side for once."

"For once?"

His *once* was strangled by the out-and-out lust that seized him as she yanked her dress over her head and tossed it on the nearest twin bed. When they'd left the house this morning, he hadn't realized she wasn't wearing a bra underneath her dress. If he had, he wasn't sure they would ever have made it out of their bedroom.

In fact, he thought with brain cells that were working at only half speed while his wife was standing in front of him in all her naked, glowing glory, at this point he wasn't sure they'd be coming out of *this* bedroom any time soon. Lori's family and friends would have to wait until he was done wringing every ounce of pleasure out of his beautiful wife.

"*Gorgeous.*"

Though he made sure to keep his hands gentle on her bare skin, he couldn't help crushing her mouth under his in a passionate kiss. She moved against him with a catlike purr, working to get closer.

"I want to see you too," she whispered breathlessly against his lips. Her fingers made short work of the buttons on his long-sleeved shirt, and she was soon shoving it off. As she ran her hands over his shoulders and then down his pectoral muscles, she gave a happy little sigh. "Talk about *gorgeous*. Maybe it's shallow of me, but I never get tired of looking at you." She grinned up at him. "Good thing I've never spent much time worrying about being shallow."

"You're the most giving person I know," he reminded her. Lori was harder on herself than anyone else. Yes, she had spunk, and spark, and could be irritating as hell. But she was never cruel or hurtful. And she gave so much more of herself than she expected from anyone else.

"Funny you should say that, because I'm in the mood to give you something I think you're really going to like. Scratch that—you're going to *love* it."

With that, she gracefully dropped to her knees, clad only in the heels he hadn't been able to convince her to give up as her pregnancy progressed. The truth was, she really could dance across a tightrope in heels.

Still, that didn't stop him from worrying. Hell, nothing could stop him from worrying. Nothing except—

The feel of her hands, and then her sweet mouth, on his erection instantly stole his thoughts away. All he could see, all he could feel was *Lori*. Her skin flushing with excitement and arousal, her tongue sliding up his hard length as though he was the most delicious treat she'd ever tasted.

On a groan that he barely remembered to muffle, he threaded his hands into her hair. Pleasure at her touch had him tightening his fingers in the strands. But instead of complaining about his rough touch, Lori only grew more excited.

He knew how much she loved to tempt him, to tease him, to break through his self-control. And it was the same for him—few things were better than when his spitfire of a wife fully let go while they were making love.

The raw sensuality of her mouth and hands on him had him nearly losing it right then and there. More than his own pleasure, however, he wanted to feel Lori's heart beating against his chest, her skin slick as it slid against his, her mouth available for him to devour as she tumbled over the edge.

Withdrawing, he bent to lift her to her feet.

"Spoilsport," was the only word he let her get out before he kissed her, claiming her mouth again with deep possessiveness.

"Later," he promised her. "I'm going to play with

you until your voice is hoarse from crying out."

"Now," she begged. "Do it now. Everyone at the party can wait."

But he was already turning them around so that she was facing the door and he was behind her. Gently, he placed her hands flat against the wood on either side of her head.

"Stay exactly like this. Don't move, or I'll stop."

"You'd have steam coming out of your ears, among other places, if you walked away from me now," she countered.

But she stayed right where she was, causing his smile to widen.

Grayson knew better than to think that Lori would ever let him control her life, her decisions, her actions—and he would never want to steal away her independence. But they both loved these moments when she gave him her trust and let him guide their pleasure.

All because she knew that nothing was more important to him than her happiness.

Not one single thing mattered more to Grayson than Lori.

Stepping back to look at her, he appreciated the strength of her shoulders, the elegance of her spine, the sweet curve of her hips—and of course, those long, luscious legs that had taken his breath away from the start.

"I don't know how you do it," he murmured as he ran his hands slowly over her bare skin. "How you grow more and more beautiful with every day that passes."

She opened her mouth to respond, but whatever words she'd been about to speak turned into a gratifying moan of pleasure when he slid one hand around from her hips to the vee between her thighs. She was so warm and so soft and so damned slick that she wasn't the only one moaning as he caressed her.

"Take me, Grayson. *Please.*" Only Lori could sound so demanding while begging.

Instead, he deliberately lowered his voice to a growl. "Is this what you wanted to show me? How good it feels when you take me in your mouth until I can't think straight, and then how good it sounds to hear you gasp and moan as you come wild and wet against my hand—"

His dirty talk had her inner muscles clenching against his fingers, tight enough that she stole the breath out from beneath the rest of his words. No longer able to tease either of them another second, he gently widened her stance with his hands on her thighs, then went down to his knees on the wooden floor.

When his mouth closed over her sex, she moaned his name, low and long. Knowing all it would take was one more swipe of his tongue, one tiny press of his thumb over her arousal, and she'd break apart, he held her just at the precipice of bliss. For a few heady moments, he paused to savor, to relish her taste, her scent, her heat.

Of course, he should have known that was when she'd take back control by rocking her hips against his mouth, a movement so small he might have missed it if he wasn't so attuned to her every breath, each throb of her heartbeat.

He lifted his mouth from her skin at the same moment that he gripped her hips. Not so hard that he'd leave marks, but firmly enough that she was yet again compelled to follow his sensual lead.

"Not so fast." He thought he heard her muffle a curse. "What was that, my darling wife?"

Though his heart was practically beating through his chest, and he was as hard as stone, he grinned when she let loose a string of curses, making it abundantly clear what she was going to do to him if he didn't make her come *right this very second*!

Another time, he might have teased her longer, knowing it would only make her release better when he finally let it come. But today was their baby shower, so he supposed he could give her one of her presents a little early.

Without warning, he slid his finger inside her slick

heat at the same moment that he played his tongue over her sex. Her orgasm came hard and raw and perfect as her hips rocked helplessly against his mouth.

He was so desperate for her that he was barely aware of getting up from the floor to press his chest against her back and put his hands over her glorious breasts to play with her extremely sensitive skin while she rubbed the curve of her bottom against his erection.

"Don't hold back," she urged him over her shoulder. "I need you, Grayson. *All* of you."

Though he was nearly as far gone as he could remember ever being, there was no way he would forget that he needed to be careful with Lori. There would be plenty of time for wild and crazy sex again in the future.

"I don't want to hurt you or the baby." He must have said it to her a hundred times during the past few months.

"You know what the doctor said," she reminded him, as she had so many times before. "As long as nothing hurts, it's fine to continue 'normal intimate relations.'"

She mimicked the doctor's voice, which usually made him laugh despite himself. But now that they were only weeks away from her due date, he couldn't laugh about it anymore.

She turned her head to capture his gaze over her shoulder. "I promise everything's going to be okay, for both me and the baby." She paused, searching his face. "When have I ever broken a promise to you?"

He blew out a harsh breath. "Never."

"And I'm not going to start today. Not even when I need you so bad that I feel like I'll detonate soon if you don't just take me already."

"It's how I feel too."

"Then take me, Grayson. *Love* me."

Between one heartbeat and the next, he was covering her mouth with his and he was taking her. Loving her.

"*Lori.*" Her name on his lips was a vow. A promise. A prayer.

"I love you, cowboy."

The smile on her lips, in her voice, in her eyes, sent his body rocketing over the edge, while her words of love brought his heart tumbling toward the kind of ecstasy he'd never known was possible.

Until Lori.

CHAPTER THREE

"I've never seen a pregnant woman look so good." Valentina gave Lori a big hug. "You're positively glowing."

Valentina was married to Lori's movie-star brother, Smith. During the past year, Valentina and Smith had married at Summer Lake in upstate New York, honeymooned in Maine, where they adopted their dog Magoo, then opened Sullivan Studios in San Francisco to produce movies and TV shows. Lori was thrilled that Valentina and Smith had decided to settle full time in the Bay Area. She'd missed her brother so much over the years when he'd been on sets all over the world filming his iconic movie roles.

"I've never felt better." As Lori said it, she couldn't keep from turning to moon over her husband, whose *very* sexy moves and loving words were wholly responsible for the current exceptional state of her glow.

Grayson was across the room chatting with Lori's brother Zach and his pregnant wife, Heather. Zach and Heather were due to have their first child in six weeks.

The two couples had discussed having a double baby shower, but given that Zach and Heather had already shared their wedding day, Lori didn't think it was fair for them to share their baby shower too. The Sullivans would all be getting together again next month to fête them.

Valentina elbowed Smith in the ribs when he remained silent and somewhat scowly. "Doesn't your sister look great?"

"You really do." Smith brushed her hair away from her face and kissed her forehead, the same big-brother kiss he'd been giving her since she was two years old. When she was a little girl, he would always watch over her while she played in the backyard to make sure she didn't hurt herself as she constantly tested her own limits. "I can't tell you how glad I am that your pregnancy is going so well."

Though Smith was considered to be one of the best actors of his generation, and should have been able to school his features, he couldn't quite prevent himself from shooting another scowl in her husband's direction.

Lori knew how much her brother liked Grayson. Still, Smith had never been particularly good at controlling his protective urges, especially when his little sister had just been drooling over her husband.

She loved few things more than razzing her brother. "In case you missed the day they did sex education in high school," Lori said in her sweetest tones, "the way a girl and a boy make a baby is—"

When Smith's hand shot out to cover her mouth, she burst out laughing. She also couldn't resist pretending to bite his fingers, which had him dropping his hand with alacrity.

"I don't know why all of my brothers have to be so predictable," she said to her cousin Cassie, who had just joined the group. "I'm *clearly* not a virgin anymore." Lori rubbed her belly to further emphasize her statement.

"Honestly," Cassie said, picking up the thread of the conversation, "I find it's easier if my four brothers still think I'm a virgin, even though that ship sailed a long, long time ago."

All of them laughed, except for Smith, who was still looking a little grumpy, probably because he had guessed why Lori and Grayson had been late to their own party. They'd emerged breathless from her bedroom down the hall with their hair and clothes slightly askew.

"Trust me, Cassie. Even your male cousins want to think that." Valentina gave Smith a little nudge. "In fact, if we're going to get any good girl talk in, maybe you should go check that Magoo isn't tearing up your mom's backyard." Almost completely blind, Smith and

Valentina's dog was as handsome and lovable a fellow as they came.

As soon as Smith was out of hearing, Valentina turned back to Lori. "From the gleam in your eyes whenever you look at Grayson, I take it everything I've heard about pregnancy hormones and increased libido is true?"

"And then some," Lori confirmed with a quintessentially naughty grin. "Take it from me, every baby shower should start with a hot quickie."

"You had sex with Grayson before the party began?" Cassie looked partly shocked. But mostly intrigued. And possibly a tiny bit envious. "Where?"

"My old bedroom."

Cassie's eyes grew even bigger. "Have I mentioned recently how much I adore you just for being you, Lori?"

"A girl can never hear it enough." Lori gave her cousin a big hug. "Just like I can never thank you enough for that ridiculously cool cake. My Instagram feed has been lighting up like the Fourth of July ever since I posted a picture of it—even now I can hear my phone in my purse, dinging away with notifications."

For their shower, Cassie had made a cake in the shape of a dancing baby girl in a cowboy hat, with cute little pigs and sheep and horses all around her. It was positively brilliant. For the millionth time, Lori wished her cousin didn't live all the way over on the other coast. Thankfully, over the years Lori had been in so many dance shows along the Eastern Seaboard that she'd been able to visit with Cassie, her other six Maine cousins, and Uncle Ethan and Aunt Beth, quite a lot.

Both Ethan and Beth were here today—they were currently chatting with Lori's mom, Uncle Max and Aunt Claudia from Seattle, and Uncle William from New York. Her cousin Hudson, a landscape architect, and Brandon, a luxury hotel mogul, hadn't been able to make it, however. Neither had Ashley, who had stayed in Maine with her son to keep watch over the family business. Lori loved the Irish cafés and gift stores that Ethan and Beth had opened throughout Maine. Time and time again, she had told them that she thought their business would do just as well on the West Coast, in the hopes that they'd expand the family business this way soon.

Fortunately, Cassie's other siblings were here. Turner was a brilliant animator who had worked on several fantastic movies and TV shows. Rory was an incredibly talented furniture maker who had made the driftwood coffee table in Lori and Grayson's living room. And Lola not only designed knockout textiles, she was also a knockout bombshell. Thankfully, she was also one of the nicest women on the planet.

Lori was endlessly proud of her cousins. Grayson

liked to joke about how many there were. Truth be told, even Lori tended to lose count once she started adding in her second and third cousins in Europe and Australia and Asia. No matter where she went in the world, family was never far away.

Lori put her hand over the spot on her belly where the baby was kicking up a storm, safe in the knowledge that her daughter would always be surrounded by people who loved her.

Realizing she must have drifted off inside her head for a few moments—something that never used to happen before she became pregnant—Lori turned back to Cassie. "When I first saw your cake, I thought it looked too good to eat. But we pregnant women are *always* hungry. And your cake is *so* good." So delicious that she couldn't resist snagging another bite from Cassie's own plate.

"I had a lot of fun coming up with the ideas for it," Cassie said with smile.

"Anything else—or *anyone*—you're having fun with recently?"

"Candy and pastry, yes. Men?" She shook her head. "Nope, not a one."

Lori raised an eyebrow. "You're not holding out on any dirty details, are you?"

"Trust me, if I had dirty details to share, you'd be one of the first people I'd tell them to. After all, no one appreciates TMI more than you."

"I'm going to hold you to that promise. In fact, there are a couple of cowboys Grayson and I know that we could—"

"No!" Cassie held up her hands, clearly horrified by what Lori was about to suggest. "I can't do setups. They always go terribly, embarrassingly wrong. Besides, you've already snagged the best cowboy around."

"I really have," Lori agreed, going all dreamy again as she looked over at her husband.

"How has Grayson been holding up during your pregnancy?" Chloe asked, joining the conversation. Married to Lori's brother Chase and mother to four-year-old Emma and two-year-old Julia, Chloe was a masterful fiber artist who had been the perfect addition to the Sullivan family from day one.

"Fortunately, my pregnancy has been perfect," Lori replied. "I haven't been sick. I haven't had any red flags. I've taken my prenatal vitamins and eaten all the right food. Apart from wearing these five-inch spikes—" She lifted up one heeled foot. "—I'm doing everything by the book. Still…" She hadn't forgotten how tense Grayson had seemed earlier. Nor had she forgotten the look of panic on his face after the dog nearly knocked her over in the kitchen. "Right after we got here, while we were saying hi to Mom, he seemed worried."

"Though sweet and wonderful, husbands aren't always rational," Chloe noted. "In fact, even though they don't mean to be, sometimes they're downright out of their minds."

"Out of their minds?" Vicki, an award-winning sculptor who was married to Lori's baseball-playing brother, Ryan, joined the group. With her was Nicola, a world-famous musician who was married to Lori's vintner brother, Marcus. "I'm assuming we're talking about your brothers, Lori?"

"Of course we are, along with my husband."

"I know they can act like cavemen," Nicola said, "but honestly—" She was blushing as she admitted, "I kind of like it when Marcus goes all Neanderthal on me."

Though there were plenty more eye rolls, Lori knew that all of them felt the same. Not one of them would trade their man for anything.

"But enough about our caveman husbands," Nicola said in an obvious bid to spin the conversation in a less blush-worthy direction. "The big question everyone wants to know is whether you and Grayson have picked a name yet."

Lori shook her head. She and Grayson had been going round and round about names ever since her pregnancy test had come back positive. But they'd yet to agree on a name. "We're probably going to be one of those couples who leave a blank space on the birth certificate for the first two weeks," she joked, even though the truth was that it *did* bother her. Why couldn't they decide on a name? Shouldn't there be at least one that felt right?

"Hi, beautiful!" Lori's cousin Mia found her way right into the center of the group to give Lori a smacking kiss on the cheek. "You look amazing, so I won't ask how you're feeling. All I want to know is, do you have a babymoon planned yet? If not, I'm going to drop everything to find you a killer vacation rental so that you and your drop-dead-gorgeous husband can get away before the little ankle-biter comes along."

"A babymoon?" Lori looked at the other women. "Is that something people actually do?"

Chloe nodded. "Chase planned a special getaway for us a couple of months before Emma was born." Lori followed Chloe's gaze across the room to where Chase was pressing a kiss to their oldest daughter's cheek and drying her tears after a game with her cousins in the backyard had likely gone a bit off the rails, as backyard games tended to do. A few moments later, Emma was smiling again and dashing off to play with her cousins.

"Jake and I could only get away for a short babymoon before we had Smith and Jackie," Sophie put in, "but it was wonderful."

For years and years, Sophie and her Irish-pub-owning husband, Jake, had been secretly in love with each other. Unfortunately, Jake hadn't thought he was good enough for Sophie, so their love had been unrequited. That is, until the night of Chase and Chloe's wedding, when neither of them could continue to ignore the attraction between them...and their one-night stand resulted in Sophie's pregnancy with their own set of twins. Now, Sophie and Jake were one of the happiest couples on the planet, and their kids were an adorable handful.

"Obviously," Grace said when Lori looked at her in question, "I didn't have a babymoon with Mason."

Grace's ex had been the scum of the earth, so this wasn't a surprise to anyone. "But before Dylan and I had Aaron, we made sure to plan a long weekend for just the two of us before the sleepless nights with a newborn began." Grace and Dylan had met when Grace had been tasked with writing a major magazine story about Lori's boat-building cousin. Mason had been only a year old when Dylan met Grace—and he had instantly fallen in love with both of them.

"I didn't have a babymoon before I had Summer either," Megan said. Her toddler son, Logan, who was the spitting image of Lori's firefighting brother, Gabe, was currently fast asleep on Megan's shoulder. "But we definitely had one before Logan made his appearance.

It's a really good idea to fill the well a bit before being awash in spit-up and diapers and—" She laughed at the look on Lori's face. "Don't worry, all the hard, stinky parts are totally worth it."

"I can deal just fine with stinky pigs, so I'm not worried about diapers or spit-up." Lori came from tough stock. If her mother could wrangle eight kids, she and Grayson could surely deal with one. "But back to this whole babymoon thing. I'm still not sure why it's such a big deal."

It wasn't until Chloe and Grace both blushed that Lori finally had her answer.

"Ahhh...so a babymoon is code for a few days of hot sex with your husband in a fancy hotel with no interruptions." She glanced over at Grayson again. No one wore a pair of jeans and cowboy boots better. "In that case, sign me up. After all, there are few things I love more than hot sex with my cowboy."

Lori's brothers Zach and Ryan had been heading toward the group of women, but after hearing the words *hot sex*, they promptly changed course for a table that was groaning with food.

"Excuse me while I go have a word with your husband to make sure this plan doesn't fall through the cracks," Mia said. "You don't mind if I drool on him while I'm over there, do you?"

Lori laughed. Few people were more outrageous

than she was, but Mia came pretty darn close. "I'm pretty sure I drooled all over Ford when he pulled out his guitar and played his new song for us at our last family get-together, so this will make us even." Though Lori would never want anyone but Grayson, that didn't mean she couldn't appreciate the appeal of her cousin's rock-star husband like any other red-blooded woman.

But before Mia could get to Grayson, he rang the bell that they normally used at home to round up the farm animals at feeding time to get everyone's attention. Though she didn't know what he was planning, when he held out his hand to her, she wound her way through the crowd to join him at his side.

"Where the heck were you keeping that cowbell?" she asked in a low voice. Her hands had been all over every inch of him before the party, so he couldn't have been storing it in his back pocket. Rather than answer, he simply kissed her, which was a more than good enough reply.

Though the adults had all come to attention, the kids were still running wild together under the watchful eyes of their close-knit family. Lori couldn't wait for her daughter to be part of the play-pack with her cousins, getting dirt in her hair and scrapes on her knees, just like Lori had while she was growing up.

"Thank you for coming here today to celebrate

with us," Grayson said, his tone deep and strong as he addressed their family and friends. "And thank you, Mary, for throwing us this wonderful baby shower." His voice sent a ripple of awareness up Lori's spine, as did the hand he used to stroke the top of her hip as he pulled her close. "Lori and I know how lucky we are to have such a great family."

While she knew that he loved spending time with her family, she also understood how overwhelming being surrounded by this many Sullivans could be. Everyone in her family had a rather strong personality, with movie stars, rock stars, pro athletes, brilliant artists, and CEOs among them. No one felt the need to brag, or lord their success over their family members. Nonetheless, a Sullivan get-together could be a lot to handle for one of their partners, and she was extremely glad that he felt so comfortable with everyone.

What's more, Grayson's parents, Gina and Brent Tyler, had flown in from New York to attend the party. The early years after he had left the East Coast to start over in California had been difficult for the three of them—not only had he left his home behind after his late wife's car accident, he'd also tried to leave every-one associated with his old home. Fortunately, when Grayson was finally ready to mend fences, his parents had welcomed him back into their lives with open arms.

Lori honestly wasn't sure they knew quite what to think of her, given that she was the polar opposite of his late wife and the society women his mother and father normally socialized with. Fortunately, as soon as they'd seen how good Lori was for their son, they had gone out of their way to be kind to her, making sure she knew how grateful they were to her for bringing their son back to them.

Grayson turned to face Lori, his heart in his eyes. "You're going to be an amazing mother." Gently, he laid his hand over her belly, and she immediately covered it with hers. "Our daughter is already so lucky to have you."

She threw her arms around him. He might be a man of few words most of the time, especially when they were in a big group, but when he did make a speech, he always brought her to tears. "I love you."

He drew her as close as he could with her belly between them. "I love you too." When they finally drew apart—to more than one teasing call to *get a room*—there was mischief in his eyes.

After everyone had clinked glasses of bubbly and called out their congratulations, Lori turned back to Grayson. "You look like you're going to burst. You haven't cooked up another surprise for me, have you?"

The first time Grayson had stunned her speechless had been on their wedding day. She'd thought they were hosting a family reunion—while everyone else was in on Grayson's real plan to marry her right then and there in the middle of their farm. Lori had said her vows to Grayson wearing her mother's wedding dress with her own cowboy boots underneath. It had been the perfect surprise. Just as the dance studio, which he'd built on their property while she'd been away with a production, had been a wonderful, unexpected gift.

Before he could reply, their mothers came over. Lori took each of their hands in hers. "It's been a fantastic baby shower, Mom. And I'm so glad you were able to be here, Gina."

"I wouldn't have missed it," Grayson's mother said, folding Lori into a hug. "And I wouldn't have believed a woman in her eighth month could look so good if I hadn't seen it for myself. I'm still marveling at how you were dancing in the backyard with the kids a short while ago, despite the fact that you've already been standing in those impossibly high heels for hours."

Now that the party had gone on long into the afternoon, Lori's feet were starting to hurt a little, along with her lower back. But it was nothing compared to the pain she'd often experienced while rehearsing for twelve hours at a stretch for a show. "Thank you for the compliment, but I've never been good at being still."

"That's for sure," Mary and Grayson said at the same moment, making all of them laugh.

"Your brothers have already helped pack away the shower gifts in the back of your SUV for you to open at home, but we have one more gift that we'd like you to open now." Gina reached into her purse and pulled out an envelope. The words *Lori and Grayson's Babymoon* were written across the front.

Lori looked up, stunned. "You're *giving* us a babymoon?" How was it that everyone but her was in on this fabulous idea?

"Your mother, Grayson, and I thought a few nights by the beach in Carmel would be the perfect way for you to relax before you have the baby. I know how busy you've been, not only with your choreography, but also taking care of your farm chores, when any other woman would have seized the opportunity to put her feet up. I know I did my fair share of resting when I was pregnant with Grayson." Gina's smile widened as she added, "Brent and I are going to head back to the farm after the party to take care of the animals, so you two don't have to worry about a thing while you're in Carmel. I'll even make sure to call the pigs by name when it's feeding time." Grayson's parents had been out to visit the farm in Pescadero enough times—and inevitably been put to work, as did anyone with idle hands—that they knew the ropes quite well by now.

"I love it!" Lori hugged all three of them at once. Her pregnancy had been great so far, and she had no doubt that this surprise babymoon was going to be the icing on the cake.

A few minutes later, Grayson went to say his thank-yous to her family, and his mother moved away to rejoin her husband by the barbecue, where Brent was doing a darned good job of grilling hot dogs and hamburgers just the way her picky little nieces and nephews wanted them. He was particularly good at slathering them in ketchup and mustard before handing them into the adorable little devils' mud-smeared hands.

Lori put her arms around her mother. "I know I say it all the time, but you really are the best mom in the whole wide world."

"You make it easy."

"I most definitely do not," Lori said on a laugh, "but I appreciate the fib. And I also appreciate that while I had never heard of a babymoon until today, I'm suddenly the lucky recipient of one! How long have you and Gina and Grayson had your heads together on this?"

"He called us a while back saying he wanted to do something special for you before the baby came— something where you would be sure to get some rest and relaxation—and hoped we might have ideas."

"Nailed it." They were going to have an amazing time at the cottage in Carmel. "I've been racking my brain trying to come up with something special for him too. Got any ideas for me?"

"All he wants is for you and the baby to be safe and sound."

Perhaps it shouldn't have been a strange thing for her mother to say. And if Mary had been speaking about someone else, Lori wouldn't have stopped to chew on it. But this was Grayson they were talking about. A man who had lost his wife in a horrible car crash three years before Lori had met him. He'd healed, but that didn't mean the scars—and the fears—from that tragedy wouldn't always be with him.

"We *are* safe and sound. Better than that, we're both thriving. I feel it with every tap dance this kid does inside of me."

"I know that," Mary said in a soft voice, "and you know that. We women have the advantage of knowing exactly how we're feeling from moment to moment during our pregnancies. But our partners have to guess from a look, or something we do or don't say."

"Do you think I need to reassure him more often that everything is okay?" Lori didn't often ask people for advice. Her mother was the rare exception. Mary Sullivan had lived such a full and amazing life. Though she never pushed her opinion on others, her hard-won wisdom was undeniable. "I know that even though he's in a much better place now than when we met," Lori continued, "sometimes his past history with his late wife comes back to haunt him and causes him to worry. But I thought, with how easy my pregnancy has been and how good I feel, that he would know everything was perfect. Have I been wrong this whole time?"

"Honey—" Her mother put her hand on her arm. "The last thing Grayson would want is for you to worry about him worrying about you. Trust me on this. What he needs most from you are your smiles and laughter and love. All the things you've always given him. All the things he's going to get twice over once your daughter is born."

Mary Sullivan was rarely—try *never*—wrong when it came to giving advice. How could she be when she'd been through it all with eight kids and a growing horde of grandkids? But Lori suddenly couldn't shake the fear that while she'd been skipping through her pregnancy, Grayson had been having a different experience entirely.

One colored by a past that she worried he might never fully be able to put to rest.

CHAPTER FOUR

During the party, Grayson had been keeping an eye on Lori, making sure she didn't wear herself out, or overdo it playing with the kids, or not get enough to eat and drink. Of course, he had to be stealthy about looking after her, or risk her coming after him with a spike heel in hand.

Lori had always been adamant about taking care of herself—and she was damned good at it. But that didn't mean he could push away his own instincts to take care of her and their baby.

Life with his wife these past years had been one adventure after another, but no adventure was bigger than having a child. He had known Lori only a week when he'd started to dream of a little girl who looked just like her, a mini-spitfire with a sparkling laugh and an indomitable spirit. Given his dark past, he'd thought they were just crazy dreams at the time, but Lori had done the impossible by making his wildest dreams an incredible—and *terrifying*—reality.

More than one person had told Grayson that he

was the calmest, steadiest man they knew. But that was only because they didn't know that inside, the thought of Lori being pregnant, of having their child, made his heart beat a million miles a minute while he barely managed to keep his breathing even. He'd thought Lori's perceptive mother might say something to him about this during the party, but thankfully Mary had held her own counsel.

Grayson knew exactly what he needed to do: suck up his fears and get the hell over them. Lori wasn't at all worried about the big changes they were facing, and he wouldn't forgive himself if he damaged that by feeding her his fears.

She'd done so much to help him face his demons over the death of his first wife. He'd sworn he wouldn't let new ones take their place. And he was going to stand by that vow, damn it.

No more lying awake at night, running over worst-case childbirth scenarios.

No more fighting back dark visions.

No more watching over Lori as though she were made of fine china, when he knew better than anyone that she had a steely determination and backbone. Especially when it came to those she cared for—there was nothing that would make her back down when it came to giving them her love.

A long weekend in Carmel couldn't have come at a

better time. Grayson desperately needed time away from the endless demands of their farm and community produce business so that he could lavish his full attention on his favorite person in the world—and show her just how much he loved her. More than anything, or anyone, else.

When Mary and his mother had suggested a babymoon—something he'd never heard of until they brought it up—he'd instantly known that Lori would love it. She celebrated even the smallest things, from the hatching of a baby chick, to a colorful sunset, to the first ear of corn growing in the field. A long weekend in a beach town was right up her alley. In addition to giving them time to connect one on one with no outside distractions, he also hoped the beach cottage would be the perfect place for Lori to relax for a few rare and uninterrupted hours.

Before they got there, however, he had one more surprise for her that he knew would be the icing on the cake of their perfect day with her family. A ballroom dancing venue was less than a mile from the coastal highway that led to Carmel-by-the-Sea. They had hit the road thirty minutes ago and were now close to the venue.

First, however, he needed to make absolutely sure that she felt up to dancing after having been on her feet the entire time at the party. Though he had literally just reminded himself not to treat her like she was breakable, he asked, "How are you feeling?"

"Really good." She turned to face him better from the passenger seat, her expression strangely serious. "What about you?" Her words seemed to hold more gravity than normal. "How are *you* feeling?"

Grayson stilled. Had she caught on to the fact that his worries were taking him over more and more with every day that passed?

No. He couldn't heap his old demons on her. Demons he thought he'd fully dealt with already, damn it!

"It was a great party." He hoped his smile didn't look strained as he said, "It means a lot that so many of the family came such a long way to celebrate with us."

"My family all adores you, Grayson." She put her hand over his, and warmth moved through him.

"I feel the same way about them." His smile came easier now as he added, "Are you glad to finally be off your feet? Maybe even ready for a nap?"

She snorted in response. "Of course I'm not ready for a nap! And my feet—" She slipped off one shoe and wiggled her painted toes. "—are always up for more action. Just like me." She waggled her eyebrows, sexy even when she was doing something silly. "What kind of action do you have in mind, cowboy?"

Though it was tempting to head straight to the cabin so that he could strip her pretty dress completely away and give her some slow-and-sexy loving *action* to counterbalance the quickie in her old bedroom, he pointed at the freeway sign. "We're right by the new ballroom and cocktail place you were telling me about last month. If you're up for it, I'd like to take you dancing."

"Yet again, you're the best husband ever!" Her eyes were bright with happiness as she leaned over and strained against her seat belt to kiss him on the cheek. "I've been *dying* to do some proper ballroom." She looked down at her stomach. "Although I'm not sure how proper I can be at this point." She shrugged. "Whatever, it's still going to be awesome to dance with you, even if everyone will be wondering the whole time if I'm about to give birth on the dance floor." She grinned. "Actually, knowing we're shocking people will make it even better."

He laughed, grateful that it eased the tightness in his chest. Soon, they were walking into the club full of people who were decked out in their best sequins and satin. And that was just the men.

"One day I'll stop being surprised by how many waxed chests there are on display in these clubs," he muttered.

"Any chance you'll unbutton your shirt?"

"No." The word was little more than a growl.

She walked her fingers up his chest. "Any chance

you'll let *me* unbutton your shirt?"

"Try it and you'll be dancing with your arms tied behind your back."

Her eyes twinkled up at him, full of mischief. "Sounds like fun."

He kissed her in lieu of groaning. And five minutes later, he was glad, yet again, for the ballroom dancing classes his parents had forced him to take when he was a teenager. For every second of those classes, he had wished he was on the basketball court instead. At fifteen, he'd been absolutely certain that he would never, ever need to know how to do the fox-trot. But even then, the universe must have known that Lori Sullivan was going to come into his life—and that he was going to need to do whatever he could to keep up with her and make her happy. Even if that meant spending time in her dance studio working on improving his posture and hold so that he could be useful to her if she needed to grab him and try out new choreography.

When they first stepped onto the dance floor, a few eyebrows rose at the sight of Lori's very round belly. But within sixty seconds, everyone's mouths were hanging wide open in awe. She was *that* good a dancer, every move she made so fluid, so effortless, so right. In fact, several people in the crowd applauded when the band came to the end of the waltz with a flourish.

"I swear," she said, her breathing still perfectly even, while he was trying to keep from panting, "you could go pro if you wanted to. You know exactly when and where to move with me—even with our baby girl bouncing between us."

He'd said it plenty of times before, and he said it again now: "The only reason I seem remotely like a good dancer is because I'm dancing with you. I guarantee there would be smashed toes and elbowed ribs if you paired me up with anyone else here."

"I know this smacks of double standards, given that I dance with other people all the time, but I don't think I could stand to let you dance with anyone else."

He drew her closer. "You're the only one I want to dance with, Lori." He lowered one hand to her stomach and grinned when he felt a good, strong kick to his palm. "Sorry, I meant the *two* of you are the only ones I want to dance with."

Lori put her hand on her belly too and laughed out loud at the feel of two little hands and two little feet pushing out. "I love that she's already dancing with us."

"Me too, sweetheart." He pressed his lips to hers and counted himself the luckiest man alive. "Me too."

CHAPTER FIVE

The cottage was both stylish and cozy, with golden hardwood floors, plush furniture in the living room and bedroom, and windows that looked out over the sweeping ocean. A storm had blown into town while they were dancing. But though they could see waves crashing on the shore and tree branches blowing back as rain lashed the windows, with the wood stove fired up, they were warm and toasty.

Grayson had pulled Lori onto his lap and wrapped a blanket around them both. A million times at least, people had told her to take it easy during her pregnancy, though they all knew that her default setting was *how-fast-can-I-go?* Moments like this were fairly rare. And only ever, she thought with a smile, because Grayson was cuddling her.

Mmmm. She *loved* cuddling with him.

Of course, she loved it even *more* when they had no clothes on.

Though her mother had cautioned Lori not to worry Grayson by worrying about him, she hadn't been able to stop herself from trying to read his emotions in the hours since they'd left the party. She hated that his demons might be trying to make a comeback.

Not on her watch, darn it!

"Do you know what this reminds me of?" She deliberately kept her voice light in the hopes that she would be able to pull him back from the brink of any darkness that might be threatening.

She was glad to feel his smile against the top of her head. "The day we were out on the horses and got caught in the storm."

"God, I *hated* you." She snuggled in closer, resting her ear against his chest so that she could hear his heart beat. Strong and steady as ever, he had given her more love than she'd ever known was possible. "At least, that's what I was trying to tell myself."

"Neither of us could pull off that lie for too long, could we?"

"Especially not once we were soaking wet and stripping off our clothes in your conveniently remote log cabin."

His callused fingers played along her bare arms, making thrill bumps dance across her skin. "I'd never known anyone bold enough to strip down in front of a virtual stranger."

"You dared me—how could I not?"

"I didn't dare you."

"We'll have to agree to disagree on that one," she said in a deceptively mild tone, before continuing, "Want to dare me now?"

"I want you to relax," he said first. Fortunately, she didn't have to wait too long for him to add, "But yes, of course I also want you to take off your clothes. I can't imagine a day will ever come when I don't want that."

"Lucky you—both of your wishes are about to come true." She slid from beneath the blanket and got to her feet. "Because I find few things more relaxing than taking my clothes off in front of you."

Heat sparked in his gaze even as an eyebrow went up. "You find stripping for me *relaxing*?"

She laughed as she reached for the hem of her dress. "Okay, so that might not be the exact right word. But that day in your cabin, even after we had been so horrible to one another, deep inside, I knew that being with you was exactly right."

With that, she pulled off her dress and tossed it across the room, standing before him in those red silk panties...and nothing else.

She could see how much effort it cost him to stay on the couch, the muscles tense in his thighs and his arms as he kept them at his sides, rather than reaching out to gently tumble her back into his lap.

Her husband was the most passionate lover imaginable. He loved nothing more than to swing her up into his arms and take her to the bed or the couch or the plush rug in front of the fireplace to smother her with kisses and caresses. Yes, he'd been gentler during her pregnancy, but the truth was that she'd come to crave their slower, sweeter lovemaking just as much as when they lit off a wild blaze of fireworks together.

Though she'd always thought that her sister and cousins and friends were incredibly beautiful during their pregnancies, she'd never thought much about what it would be like for her own body to change. And what a change it was! From having the rock-hard abs of a dancer to having no abs at all had been strange at first. But on the other hand, she'd immediately and unabashedly loved her new curves. Unsurprisingly, Grayson loved them too.

On another night, she might have teased him by doing a sexy dance to drive him crazy before she let him touch what he was drooling over. But their ballroom dancing—the way he'd moved so well, had held her so lovingly, that he'd thought of taking her there in the first place because he knew how much fun she'd have—had already been the hottest foreplay imaginable. Quickly shimmying out of her panties, she straddled him on the couch.

"So damned beautiful." He murmured the words against her lips, then whispered kisses over her cheekbones and against her neck. "How did I ever get so lucky?"

"We both did." She gasped out the final word as he found her breasts with his mouth, laving the taut tips with his tongue, then using his lips and teeth to send her reeling from pure sensation.

"I've been dying to taste you." The rawness of his tone was as potent to her as his kisses. "All day, I've been fantasizing about this." Gently laying her back against the couch pillows, he knelt over her, her legs spread wide beneath him. "Dreamed about having you naked and open to me."

They'd already made love twice—once slow and sweet just as they were waking that morning in Pescadero, and then the breathless quickie in her old bedroom in Palo Alto. And yet, Lori knew exactly how he felt. It wasn't enough. It could *never* be enough.

She was as hungry for him as he was for her. Filled with a sensual hunger that she knew would never come anywhere close to being sated.

"I'm yours, Grayson. *Always.*"

A flash of heat in his dark eyes was the last thing she saw before he put his mouth to her breast again. The most wonderful hit of pleasure had her closing her eyes and arching her back. She could explode from this alone, just from his hands and mouth on her breasts.

But when he moved lower, pressing kisses down

over her stomach, and then lower still to where she was desperate and aching for his touch, his hunger was evident in every lash of his tongue over her sex, in the thrust of his fingers inside of her, in the way he cupped her hips with his hands to bring her even closer to the edge of bliss.

She had no idea what she'd done to find the best husband on the planet—one who was not only handsome and sweet, but who also had *serious* moves in the sack. Karma clearly thought she deserved ecstasy, and of course she was happy to grab it with both hands. Which was exactly what she did as she threaded her fingers into Grayson's hair at the same moment he used his big, work-roughened hands to keep her from wiggling beneath him.

She loved the small tug of war that ensued, especially when letting him win this round meant having the orgasm of a lifetime. A climax that started from the very tips of her toes, then took over every cell in her body, until his mouth and hands had turned her into a deliriously happy—and extremely satisfied—woman.

As a dancer, Lori had excellent control of her body. Yet, when Grayson made love to her, she was often surprised to find herself suddenly in a new position, too dizzy with lust and arousal to realize that he had shifted them around. When she opened her eyes now, it was to find his wonderfully muscled body beneath hers as she straddled his hips.

Still more than a little dazed from the pleasure he'd sent coursing through her, she looked down at his tanned skin. "When did you take off your clothes?"

"It took you a while to catch your breath." He looked extremely pleased by this fact.

"It's going to take you longer," she promised.

His sexy-as-sin grin flashed, sending her heart racing all over again. "I sure hope so."

And then he lifted her hips, moved her over him, and slid inside—one perfect thrust that stole away the breath she'd only just gotten back.

Ohhhhh yes.

There was nothing she loved more than making love with her husband. Watching the rise and fall of his chest as he gave them both such epic pleasure. Drinking in the heat in his eyes as he watched her move over him, with him. Feeling the rough sensation of his hands sliding over her skin, always knowing just where to touch her so that she begged for *moremoremore*.

She'd never had a better partner—on the dance floor, in bed, in life—and every ounce of her love poured from her body to his as they did the sexiest dance imaginable with each other. His abs flexed, the ridges deep between each one as he lifted up to put one hand on her cheek and kiss her.

Both the passion and the pure, sweet love in his

kiss sent her flying over the edge into another magnificent climax, one that took him with her, his release as wild and rapturous as hers.

Lying replete in each other's arms, they dozed together on the couch. She might have slept through until morning if she hadn't smelled the most delicious food cooking.

Sitting up slightly, she brushed her hair out of her face and rubbed her hand over her eyes, before purposefully sniffing the air. "Is that chicken pot pie?"

"Sure is." While she'd napped, he had pulled on jeans. Still shirtless, he brought over a tray full of her favorite foods. Not only pot pie, but also potato salad and corn on the cob. "I asked the rental company for the name of a caterer," he explained. "She left this for us in the fridge, so all I had to do was heat it up."

"You think of everything." Sitting up naked on the couch, she pulled the blanket around herself, then took a bite of the pot pie. "Mmmm. This is so good."

"I couldn't let you and the baby go to bed hungry." She thought she saw a flash of darkness in his eyes, as though even the thought of their being left wanting hurt him. But then he smiled and said, "Especially after the workout we've given each other today."

Though he had worked to cover the dark flash quickly, Lori knew it was long past time for her to ask him if everything was okay—and remind him that he shouldn't feel he needed to hide any doubts or fears that he might have about becoming parents. They were a team, and she always wanted to support him as much as he supported her.

But before she could say any of that, he asked, "Has today made you happy, Lori?"

Her heart squeezed as she looked into his eyes. "Even if it hadn't already been the best day ever—which it most definitely was—when I'm with you, no matter what we're doing, I'm always happy."

He had done so much to make this the perfect beachside retreat—the perfect day full stop, complete with dancing and family. And now, she hated to spoil the moment with difficult questions that probed into his painful past. That would bring up things she knew he wished could be forever left alone.

She vowed to do whatever it took tomorrow morning to make sure her husband no longer harbored any fears for her or their baby. But for tonight, she truly believed the very best thing she could do for Grayson was to show him exactly how happy he made her.

Pushing her food aside, she moved onto his lap. "Want to play a game by the fire?"

He stroked her cheek. "What kind of game do you have in mind?"

She whispered something *very* naughty into his ear.

And when he kissed her as she laughed, he easily took her breath away all over again.

Although, truth be told, even when he wasn't kissing her, she never stopped feeling breathless around him.

And she knew that she never would.

CHAPTER SIX

Morning dawned sunny and bright, with clear blue skies outside the bedroom window. As she frequently did, Lori was using Grayson as a full-body pillow. Her face would have looked perfectly serene as she slept, were it not for the hint of wickedness that never quite disappeared.

Though he didn't want to wake her when he knew how much she needed the extra rest—regardless of how much energy she insisted she had—he couldn't keep from running his hand down the smooth skin of her spine in a long, soothing stroke. Not only because it made her move like a cat beneath his touch in her sleep, but also to soothe *himself.* More and more, he needed to reassure himself that she was perfectly okay and that the baby growing inside her was healthy too.

Grayson knew plenty of people had worse pasts— dark histories that were nearly impossible to recover from. With Lori's help, he *had* recovered.

At least, he thought he had, until she'd told him she was pregnant, and suddenly it had felt like his past was strangling him again. Fears of losing another loved one—or two, God forbid—were waking him up in a cold sweat in the middle of the night on a regular basis. Fortunately, Lori slept hard and rarely woke before morning, so he'd been able to keep it from her.

Just as he had so many times over the past months, he schooled himself to think straight and to remember that his life on the farm with Lori was nothing like his life in New York City. He'd come a long way, learning not only how to love with his whole heart, but also how to *compromise* with a woman who liked the sound of that word even less than he did, but did it all the same to make him happy.

But over the past few weeks, none of those rationalizations worked anymore, not when every time he closed his eyes...

He gritted his teeth, wishing he knew how to stop his fears from running away with him. He'd tried to work them out of his head by getting up extra early to start his farm duties and coming in late. He'd tried to sweat them out in their home gym, lifting increasingly heavy weights. He'd even tried to meditate them away, courtesy of the skills he'd gained when Lori had insisted they try out the new yoga studio in downtown Pescadero, which had set up business next door to the general store.

Unfortunately, nothing kept him from lying awake,

Lori in his arms, as he tried to convince himself that he wasn't going to lose everything again.

On a contented sigh, she rolled over so that he was spooning her. "Good morning, husband."

"Good morning, wife." He had to work like hell to make sure his voice didn't betray the darkness roiling inside of him.

"How about we make it a *really* good morning?" Without waiting for his response, she reached back to stroke the one part of his body that couldn't have cared less what was going on inside his head, not with Lori's soft and supple body pressed against him.

"Sure you're not worn out from yesterday?"

She opened one eye and looked over her shoulder at him, a teasing look of disdain on her face. "Worn out by having sex four times? You do know who you're in bed with, don't you?"

He laughed softly, the tightness in his chest easing. He'd always loved sparring with Lori, even when he'd been lying to himself about his feelings for her. From the moment she'd literally crashed into his life, he'd been a million times happier with her than he could ever be without.

Without.

His chest started to tighten again at the thought of something happening to her, but thankfully, the brush of her hips against his shifted his focus back to the warm, naked woman in his arms.

"Remember that day we didn't leave the bed?" She moved her hips in a slow circle against his. "Morning until night, we must have tried every position on the planet."

"What were your favorites?" He certainly had a few that he was dying to repeat.

"*All* of them!"

He laughed again, the sound hoarse as he cupped one of her breasts, lightly stroking the sensitive skin. When he found the taut tip and pinched it gently, he earned a sound of pleasure from his wife.

"How does this feel?" He already knew what her answer would be, but he loved hearing her say it.

"*So good.*"

"Only good?" He moved to her other breast, giving it the same sensual attention. "I must need to work harder." He pressed his erection against her, going for a joke so bad he knew she would love it. "*Much* harder."

Her laughter lifted him even further from the darkness.

"It's a good thing you chose farming over comedy, cowboy."

"You're the only one I want to make laugh," he agreed. Then he slipped his hand from her breasts down over her belly and into the vee between her legs. "And the only one I want to make come."

She was already so hot and wet and ready for him that he could barely keep from taking her. Not that she would have any problem with a blisteringly fast orgasm. But this morning, he wanted to stay wrapped around her warmth as long as he possibly could.

Because once he had to let the real world in...

Steeling himself against the fears that were, even now, trying to infiltrate his head and heart, he focused one hundred percent of his attention on the feel of Lori's aroused, damp skin, on the desperate little sounds she was making as she rocked into his fingers, on her clean, sweet scent, on the way she was always so open, so happy, so confident and secure in every part of herself, body and soul.

She turned her head over her shoulder, and the moment he captured her mouth, she shattered against his hand, her body trembling from the power of her orgasm, then shaking even harder when he slid two fingers inside, finding the spot that always turned her limbs to jelly.

He'd expected her to need some recovery time...but he should have known better. At eight months pregnant, Lori remained a wildcat in bed, her hand coming around to grip his rock-hard shaft, her thigh lifting so that she could position him right where she wanted him.

He didn't need further hints, or encouragement,

before thrusting deep. With one hand on her hip, he held her there for a long moment, letting her feel what she did to him, how desperate she made him.

Finally, they began to move again, her hips dancing with his. They had always been a perfect pairing, and yet their rhythm was never better than when they were making love.

The sounds of the waves crashing outside and their ragged breathing formed the soundtrack to their sweetly fierce lovemaking as they both reached the fever peak...then went tumbling over into ecstasy together.

★ ★ ★

"This is the *best* babymoon ever." Lori rolled over to prop herself up on one elbow so that she could drool over her extremely handsome husband. When the muscles just below her stomach tightened, she shifted into a more comfortable position. "We should do this every time we have a baby."

He blanched so quickly that she almost missed it, but after months of telling herself she was imagining things—and then keeping her difficult questions to herself last night—his tanned skin going pale was one troubling reaction too many.

Lori knew Grayson wanted to trust her with absolutely everything, but in order to be fully honest with her, he would need to be fully honest with himself first.

"Which part of what I just said freaked you out?"

He shook his head, obviously trying to push her concern away, just as he had so many times before. "I'm fine."

"No one should just be *fine* after sex that good." She put her hand over his chest and swore she could feel his heart skip a beat, even as her lower abdomen twinged again. It was a slightly weird feeling, one that hadn't come before in her pregnancy. "What's going on inside your head, cowboy?"

He remained silent, long enough that she actually had to bite her tongue to stop herself from prodding him. Whenever someone poked at her emotional wounds, she closed up like a clam. Though Grayson sometimes needed a little push, they were similar enough in that way that he wouldn't appreciate a shove. No matter how much it looked like he might need one.

The silence had drawn out long and heavy by the time he finally replied, "Every time."

She blinked at him, trying to figure out what those two words could mean. Because they obviously did mean something big and bad to him. Otherwise, he wouldn't have sounded so hoarse.

And gosh darn it, she wished she could figure out how to get more comfortable on the bed so that these darned twinges in her stomach would stop! Right now, she needed to focus every last ounce of her attention on her husband.

Her voice was gentle as she asked, "Every time…?"

"Every time we have a baby. That's what you just said. *We should do this every time we have a baby.*" He'd scrunched his eyes closed as he spoke, almost as though the words pained him too much to look at her as he said them. "I'm barely holding it together for *this* baby, let alone *more* babies in the future."

She could hear, could see, could feel, how much this admission cost him—her amazingly strong husband, whose shoulders carried such heavy physical weight every single day on their farm.

Had he been carrying an even heavier emotional weight for the past eight months without her knowing it?

Lori thought about what her mother had said at the baby shower—*All he wants is for you and the baby to be safe and sound*—and felt as though her heart was breaking. Why hadn't she seen this sooner?

And why did her body have to decide to knock her with so many of these darned Braxton-Hicks "practice" contractions all of a sudden?

"Grayson." She put her hand on his jaw, waiting until he opened his eyes and looked at her again. "Talk to me. Tell me what's going on. *Please.*"

He gritted his teeth, a muscle jumping in his jaw, a faint sheen of sweat appearing on his skin. "I'm freaking out."

"Because of what happened to Leslie?" She wasn't afraid to speak of his late wife, and though it hadn't been easy for him at first, over the years he'd been able to speak more freely about her too. At least until now.

"Yes." He grimaced. "No." He cursed, running a hand over his face. "I can see how healthy you are. I'm there at every doctor visit and hear the nurse and obstetrician say how well your pregnancy is going. And when I feel our daughter give a good, strong kick against my hand, I know better than to let the darkness come back." He paused, let out a harsh breath. "But it's been coming anyway."

"It's normal to be scared," she said softly. "This whole baby thing we're doing...it's a big deal."

"Not scared." The look in his eyes seared her. "*Terrified.*"

She swallowed hard, his *terrified* echoing around inside her head, even as her stomached ached more and more. But she didn't have time to focus on that now, not when Grayson needed everything she had to give him.

"I've been so blind." Her words were hollow as she realized just how badly she'd let him down during her pregnancy. "How could I not see what you've been feeling? What you've been going through? My pregnancy, our baby—I knew it would bring up your fears, even the ones it seemed you had finally put to rest. But apart from the fact that you've been more overprotective than usual, I thought you were okay."

"Lori—"

She gripped his hands tightly, wishing she could rewind back to the day when she'd taken the pregnancy test and seen the word *Pregnant* on the digital screen, wishing she could do things differently, wishing she could be there for him and keep him from going through this pain. "I shouldn't have missed your worries—but I've been so wrapped up in my changing body, and how the baby is growing, and my excitement and happiness over starting our own family, that I completely steamrolled over your feelings. Almost like I thought my confidence could erase any fears that rose to the surface for you. When all along, I should have been taking care of you the way you've always taken care of me."

"Sweetheart—"

"I'm the *worst* wife ever," she moaned.

"No, you're the *best* wife ever." He tugged on their connected hands to bring her closer. "Don't you know this is one of the reasons I love you so much? Because you are always full of boundless confidence, even in the face of something truly terrifying like a little person who will depend entirely on us."

"Before either of us says anything more, I want you to know that I'm *really* hoping you'll say that I'm the *best wife ever* again at some point so that I can record it. Otherwise, no one will ever believe me." Even in the heavy moments, Lori believed lightness had its place. If for no other reason than as a reminder that there were brighter times to come. "But what I really want you to know is that I trust you with everything, Grayson. With my heart, my soul, my life. And if you can live with me, if you can take care of me and my endless list of life requirements, then a baby will be no sweat."

She wished for even the slightest upturn of his mouth, but her hopes were dashed when he remained quiet. She wanted to say more, wanted to try to convince him in any way she could that everything would be okay. That the past wouldn't repeat itself. That he wouldn't lose another loved one. But where she was liable to shoot off her mouth without thinking things through, he liked to take the time to collect his thoughts, especially when they were talking about something this important.

"Once upon a time," he finally said, "you told me you came to my farm because I needed you to keep me from withering away in my grief. To help me have a future. I tried to push you away, and I said awful things that weren't true—"

"Some of them were true." He'd accused her of hiding out on his farm, rather than facing up to her own problems.

"No. *None* of the horrible things I said were true. You needed time, and space, away from your normal life to figure out how to move forward. And that's exactly what you did. You figured out how to heal your past so that you could create an amazing future. Thank God you wanted me in that future."

"I wouldn't have gotten there without you." She nearly stumbled over her words as the pinching sensation in her stomach came again, harder and longer this time. "That night you brought me to the barn dance and dared me to get out on the floor—only you could have showed me that my passion for dancing hadn't gone anywhere."

"I might have given you a few shoves in the right direction, sweetheart, but I don't have one single doubt that you would have gotten there on your own. Whereas, without you in my life..." He shook his head, his eyes going black again. "You have always understood me better than anyone else, Lori. And you have always known exactly how to reach me when I don't want to let anyone in."

"So then, why haven't you told me what you've been feeling these past months? Why haven't you shared with me how deep your fears have been running? Why haven't you let me try to help?"

"Because I didn't want to admit it to myself." She laid one hand over his chest and felt how hard his heart was pounding. "I thought loving you was the scariest thing I would ever do, that it was the biggest risk imaginable. But a baby?" His breath came fast as he said, "I can still hardly believe that we're going to have a child."

"It's going to be *amazing*! Our daughter is going to be the best thing that's ever happened to us."

"I know she will be."

And she could hear, could feel, that he truly did believe that. If only that belief weren't buried under so many of his worries that something, anything, might go wrong in the future for Lori or their child.

Now that her blinders were finally off, she could see that his demons were riding him *hard*, especially now that she was so close to her due date.

Though Grayson was a surprisingly eloquent man, he was a man of action first and foremost. Trying to talk this through might help him take a tiny step in the right direction, but he was right when he'd said that she knew exactly how to reach him.

Staying inside and debating the validity of his fears wasn't going to do it. In the past, it had been a magic combination of laughter and fun and *love* that had pulled him out of the darkness. She was hopeful they could work their magic on him yet again.

"Come on." Taking his hand, she pulled them both out of bed. "We're going out."

CHAPTER SEVEN

Grayson heard barking dogs first. Happy cries of children—hordes of them, it seemed—sounded moments after.

He rubbed the back of his neck. He didn't actually have whiplash, but the way Lori could change tack so quickly often made him feel like it.

He'd learned by now not to question her. Okay, that wasn't strictly true. He couldn't help himself most of the time, not when she was so damned fun to tease. But this morning, he was definitely not in a teasing mood.

Not now that she knew the truth—that he was barely hanging on by his fingernails.

He hadn't meant for his fears to come spilling out like that. He hadn't wanted to face his own feelings, let alone explain them to his wife in excruciating detail.

But most of all, he didn't want her to blame herself in any way for any part of his behavior. He never wanted her inner light to be diminished by anyone, or anything. Especially him. Which was why he'd immediately stopped her from berating herself over not seeing what a mess he was.

And yet, now that he'd finally unloaded some of his worries, he couldn't deny that he felt a little lighter. It might be because they were outside on a sunny beach. And because of the joy on Lori's face as she sat on the sand playing with a rambunctious, and very cute, litter of puppies.

Whatever the reason, he would gladly take the respite for as long as it lasted.

Still, when he realized they were surrounded by at least two dozen dogs, cats, rabbits, and guinea pigs—and approximately one hundred elementary school-children—he had to ask, "What have you gotten us into this time?"

"Remember that store I went into during my third, or maybe it was my fourth, bathroom break during the drive here yesterday?" During the past few months, Lori claimed the baby wasn't just sitting on her bladder, she was dancing a jig on it. "I found a flyer for this pet-adoption event put on by the local elementary school." She winced slightly when one of the puppies climbing over her jabbed her skin with its needlelike toenails. "I thought it would be fun to pitch in." She reached up to touch his hand. "Sound good?"

Lori rarely asked him if he was on board with one of her plans—she just railroaded him into participating.

Clearly, the fact that she was checking in about it meant that she was really concerned about him.

He got down on the sand with her and the puppies. "Anything that makes you smile works for me."

"*Anything?*" Just like that, the mischievous twinkle in her eyes was back.

He pretended to groan as he said, "Well..."

"No take backs." She picked up the smallest puppy of the group and gathered him close to her chest. "This little guy makes me smile. Wait—" She lifted the dog to check out its undercarriage. "Yup, he's a he. And I would really love to take him home with us."

Grayson knew there was no point in reminding her that they already had loads of animals on their farm— or that they were also going to be taking care of a baby soon too. By way of answering, he said, "You've already named him, haven't you?"

"Of course I have," she said, her smile even bigger now. "His name is Carmelo. Carmelo Sullivan-Tyler."

Grayson's chest, though still a little tight, felt increasingly better as he reached out for the tiny dog of indeterminate breeding. Lori grimaced slightly as she handed the puppy over, which normally would have jump-started Grayson's worrying again. But after their talk this morning, he knew he needed to turn over a new leaf. Most likely, he told himself, it was simply because she didn't want to let go of the puppy so soon.

"You stay here on the sand and play with the puppies. I'll take this little guy over to the adoption desk and make it official. Although he doesn't look old enough to take home yet." He studied the puppy's paws and muzzle. "I'm guessing we'll be able to pick him up in about three weeks."

"A baby and a puppy at the same time." Lori beamed. "How perfect!"

Grayson knew plenty of people—make that *most* people—would disagree with her on that score. But he knew that she truly meant it. As far as his extremely energetic wife was concerned, the more activity and fun and excitement in her life, the better. Even if it meant dealing with dirty diapers *and* puppy accidents on too little sleep.

As he carried the puppy over to the adoption table that had been set up on the sand, the puppy kept trying to lick his face. No matter how he repositioned him, the little furball scampered back up Grayson's chest and planted another wet puppy kiss on his cheek.

Though Grayson wasn't the world's biggest fan of dog breath, Carmelo's persistence was pretty darned adorable. It didn't hurt that Lori had finally picked a good name for one of their animals.

It never got any less weird to see the pigs come running for their feed when she called out, *Marcus, Chase, Ryan, Sophie*. As for their cat, Milliebob? Well, that had to be one of the worst names in creation, a crude combination of the names they'd each chosen for their rescue cat.

"Would you like to adopt this handsome fellow?"

"Yes." Grayson handed over the puppy to the woman from the local pet shelter so that she could check his tags. The puppy whined until the lady handed him back, then happily snuggled into the crook of Grayson's arm and closed his eyes. Snuffling snores sounded less than sixty seconds later.

"Please fill out this paperwork. Once we've checked that everything looks good—" Grayson appreciated that this pet rescue took the time to make sure their animals were going to good homes. "—we will give you a call to let you know when you can come pick him up at the shelter. He's got another few weeks to go before he's fully weaned."

"Sounds good." Holding the puppy on one arm, Grayson filled out the adoption application. "In addition to adopting the puppy, my wife and I came today to see if you could use some extra volunteers."

The woman looked even more pleased. "We'd really appreciate the help. Honestly, the most important thing is to make sure people get a chance to meet the animals. Especially the ones that aren't as obviously adorable as your new puppy." She stroked the soft fur on Carmelo's head. "If you and your wife—who I'm assuming is the stunning woman playing with the other puppies—would like to join me, I'll take you on a tour of some of the animals we need to go the extra mile with to increase their odds of adoption."

For the next fifteen minutes, Lori was in heaven meeting the different animals. A cat with three legs. A blind rabbit. A guinea pig missing most of the fur on its back.

Without being told, Grayson knew Lori wanted to adopt them all. Honestly, he was tempted too. More than tempted, in fact. But as their farm really was full to the brim, he hoped there were other families here today who would take these animals home and love them the way they deserved to be loved.

Just the way Lori had always loved him.

★ ★ ★

Lori didn't normally second-guess herself. Once she made a decision, she moved boldly and confidently.

But she couldn't stand the thought of Grayson being unhappy. Particularly when they were on the verge of the most wonderful thing ever to happen to them.

Soon, they were going to have a baby. A little girl who was going to have the best daddy in the entire world—one who would always put her first and who already loved her to the moon and back.

The muscles in Lori's back tightened again, a beat

before the pain inched around the front toward her belly button. Both sharp and lingering, her contractions had definitely ratcheted up during the past hour.

When she'd been lying in Grayson's arms after making love this morning, she'd been able to convince herself that they were nothing more than Braxton-Hicks "practice" contractions. But with each passing pain since, she'd started to wonder if she might not actually be given much practice before having their baby.

Still, as Grayson finally looked at ease while chatting with prospective adoptees about the charming and friendly personality of the three-legged cat, she wasn't about to let him know that there was a teeny, tiny chance she might be going into labor three weeks early. Not yet, anyway. Not when the darkness that had been hovering over him was dissipating more and more with every animal he helped to find a new home, and with the joy and laughter of the kids playing on the beach.

Hopefully, their little girl would hold her horses for just a while longer, until Grayson had found some measure of peace. Because if Lori really was in labor, that newfound peace was exactly what he was going to need to get him through.

★ ★ ★

Grayson couldn't take his eyes off a little girl who was no more than five or six. She looked so much like the picture Mary Sullivan had given him of Lori when she was that age: pigtails flying, missing a front tooth, her cheeks pink with excitement as she met the animals one by one. Though she was a ball of energy, she was extremely gentle with the animals, especially the older ones.

"She's cute, isn't she?" Lori looked up from where she'd been working her magic by convincing a couple that they absolutely *had* to take a brother and sister pair of Chihuahuas. "I keep wondering what our daughter is going to be like. Is she going to be a little spitfire like me, or quiet like Sophie? Or maybe she'll be creative like Cassie? Or a wiz at business like Mia? Or maybe a brilliant brain like Suzanne?"

"Whatever her personality, she's going to be perfect."

Lori gave him a smile so big, his chest ached with love for her. Then she winced again, a flash of pain clear enough that he couldn't blame sharp puppy nails or lightly nipping teeth.

"Lori—?"

But then, out of the corner of his eye, he saw the little girl reach out to pet a small white dog at the exact moment that a bull terrier, who had to weigh at least eighty pounds, went chasing after a ball...and knocked the girl's feet out from under her.

Grayson leaped into action, trying to get to her before she could hit the sand. Without superhuman speed, however, he didn't stand a chance.

His heart thudded painfully in his chest when he saw how hard she went down, though sand had thankfully cushioned her fall.

Kneeling at her side a few moments later, he asked, "Are you okay?"

She blinked up at him as though he was crazy. "Why wouldn't I be?"

"You just fell."

"I fall all the time." And then, "Are you a superhero?"

"No." Not even close. "Why?"

"You kind of look like one."

With that, she got up and skipped away, not the slightest bit bothered by an accident that would have had any other child on the beach bawling their eyes out.

Still staring after the girl, marveling at how she hadn't so much as missed a beat, he didn't realize Lori had come to kneel beside him until she said, "You're wrong, you know." She put her hand on his cheek. "You are a superhero. *My* superhero."

She kissed him, then looked back toward the girl. "Resilient little thing, isn't she? I'm tempted to ask her if she wants to join my dance troupe."

That was when it hit him. *"Resilient."* He turned to face Lori. "You're resilient."

Now it was her turn to look at him as though he had a screw loose, so reminiscent of the little girl's expression that he might have laughed.

"That's right. I am."

"Leslie wasn't." Wanting Lori to understand, he explained, "Back when Leslie and I met in college, she was already pretty fragile. She had a huge heart, but she wasn't up for many risks. And when life only got harder...well, you know what happened."

"I'll never stop wishing I could have met her and thanked her for loving you."

Time and time again, Lori showed him it was okay to revisit the past with both tears *and* laughter. She had not only healed his broken heart—she'd made it whole again.

He reached for her hand to help her to her feet. "That little girl reminded me so much of you. Most of all when she got up and skipped off as though she hadn't just crashed to the ground moments earlier. You're so resilient that I can finally see that our daughter will be too. All this time, I shouldn't have been worrying. Because you're stronger than anyone else I've ever known, Lori. Even if life sometimes knocks you down, you're going to get right back up again."

"You're resilient too, Grayson."

Her words made him stop to think about whether it was true. But he didn't need to do that, did he? Not when he knew that Lori only ever spoke the truth.

What's more, he finally saw why she had decided to bring him to this pet adoption on the beach in the middle of their intense discussion. She had wanted to remind him of all the wonders of life and the beauty in absolutely everything.

"You're right." It had taken him far too long to realize that for every ounce of pain and hurt in his past, there was far, far more love and laughter in his present and future. "Whatever happens, I'm not going to lose it."

She let out a sigh of relief. "I can't tell you how glad I am that you've finally realized that I'm right about everything." She winked. "Especially this."

Then she winced again.

Regardless of his innate resilience, his heart couldn't help but squeeze tight in his chest. "Lori, what's wrong?"

"Absolutely nothing." Her smile was sunnier than ever. "In fact, you know how I told my mom at the party that I wished we didn't have to wait three more weeks to meet our baby? Well, it looks like my wish is coming true." She pointed at the small puddle on the sand between her feet. "My water just broke. We're having our baby today."

CHAPTER EIGHT

"Do you need me to drive?" Lori asked.

Grayson sat frozen behind the steering wheel, the engine idling in the parking lot. "No, you're in labor. I should drive."

"Cool," she said in the lightest voice she could manage when a massive contraction was currently gripping her stomach and back and every other part of her it could reach. Waiting until she thought she might be able to speak again without the words coming out through clenched teeth, she finally said, "Then maybe we should head to the hospital now."

But instead of putting the car in gear, he said, "This wasn't the plan. We have everything arranged with the hospital at UCSF. You love your obstetrician there. We have a birth plan."

Sophie had warned her about how even the calmest man tended to lose it once labor started. Actually, many of her sisters-in-law and cousins had told her the same thing—their strong, steady husbands had fallen apart when they'd given birth to their first child.

"I love that already our daughter doesn't play by the rule book and is ready to come a few weeks before her due date." Lori put her hand over Grayson's and squeezed it. "I'm not sure, however, that it means she needs to be born in a car." She hit the button on his phone that would give them the directions to the nearest hospital in Monterey as they drove. "Just do what the nice robot voice says, and we should be there in thirty minutes."

Thankfully, he finally put the car in gear.

She hoped a half hour would be fast enough. Sure, having a baby in a car in Carmel would be a heck of a story to tell. But though she'd always been a showman, Lori would be perfectly happy to toe a more tried-and-true line with doctors and nurses nearby when it came to giving birth to her first child.

Not, of course, that she was planning on saying *any* of that to Grayson. Though he'd had a great epiphany about resilience on the beach, there was no need for the universe to force his hand this quickly. A nice, easy, simple birth would be fantastic. For both of them.

She couldn't help laughing out loud at the thought. So few things in her life had been *nice*, *easy*, or *simple* that it was preposterous to think her labor and delivery would fall under any of those categories.

As if to prove her right, another contraction hit, morphing her laughter into a groan.

"Lori?" Grayson nearly slammed on the brakes.

"I'm fine." She puffed the words out in the Lamaze breathing rhythm that she'd learned during the prenatal classes she and Grayson had attended. "Just keep driving."

Though she'd intended to be as stoic as possible, she needed to grab his arm and clamp down tight to make it through the next contraction.

"Don't worry, sweetheart." Grayson's voice was suddenly strong and clear again. She'd been the steady one in her pregnancy up until now, but from the renewed strength in his voice, she knew that it was now okay for her to fall apart. Her husband would be there to pick up the pieces if she needed him to. "I'm going to get you to the hospital with plenty of time to spare. Everything is going to be fine."

"I know." And despite the brutal pain now coming at ninety-second intervals, she truly believed him. As always, she'd never felt safer, or in better hands.

Using the car's hand free speaker, he called the hospital. He calmly explained that they were five minutes away and that she was having near-constant contractions. When the administrator asked for more information, before either of them could give it, Lori was hit with the most overpowering pain so far.

Her moans said it all. The administrator informed them that an obstetric nurse would be waiting out front.

Lori closed her eyes on the next contraction and didn't open them again until they were parked in front of the hospital and Grayson was helping her into the wheelchair the hospital had provided. By the time the nurse had wheeled her inside the maternity ward, Grayson had supplied Lori's name, age, expected due date, and other vital information.

"As soon as you're up on the bed, we'll see how far along you are." The nurse was cheerful, but thankfully not in a fake way that made Lori want to punch her. She had obviously been doing this for many years. It was comforting to know that whatever happened today, this nurse would have seen it and handled it before.

Grayson had barely finished helping Lori strip out of her clothes, put on the hospital smock, and get onto the bed, when a sound she'd never thought she'd make came out of her mouth. It hadn't hurt this bad when she'd broken her arm at fifteen and the bone had come through her skin!

The nurse nodded as she took a quick look. "Looks like your baby is ready to say hello." She pulled off her gloves, then reached for the phone on the wall. "Could you please let the doctor know we're ready for him in room four?"

"We're about to meet our little girl." Grayson's

hands over hers felt like they were the only things tethering her to the earth. "I love you so much, Lori."

She wanted to tell him she loved him too, wanted to thank him for giving her more happiness than she'd ever dreamed of. But as another contraction hit—one that made her want to bear down like nobody's business—what came out instead was a string of curses.

"You sound just the way I did when I had my three daughters," the nurse said, a hint of laughter—and empathy—in her voice.

"*Three?*" Though gritting her teeth, Lori couldn't hold back her incredulous response. "You willingly did this three times?" Sure, she'd often talked about having a house full of kids. But that was before she had felt *this*.

"I know it might be hard to believe right now, but I promise it's all worth it. Ah, here's the doctor."

"Hello, Lori, Grayson. I'm Dr. Mishrani." The man had a warm, friendly smile that instantly comforted her, despite the searing discomfort she was in. "How are you feeling?"

"Like I'm being torn in two!"

Grayson gripped her hands tighter and pressed a kiss to her forehead. "You're so strong, Lori. The strongest person I know. You can do anything. And I'm going to be here for you every single second."

She'd never appreciated the warmth of his touch,

the rock-steady confidence in his gaze, more than she did now, when she needed it most. And yet, she still couldn't keep from begging the doctor, "Please make the pain stop!" She'd once danced the final half of *The Nutcracker* with two broken toes. That had been *nothing* compared to this.

Settling onto the stool between her feet, the doctor did a quick check. "You are fully dilated and ready to push, which means that you will be feeling much better very soon. In fact, the next time a contraction comes, I want you to bear down with all your might for five seconds, which I will count down for you. Okay?"

Already feeling everything inside of her tighten and cramp, without replying, she started to push for all she was worth.

"*One.*"

Lori swore nothing had ever been so hard before!

"*Two.*"

Why had she thought having a baby would be no big deal?

"*Three.*"

She was going to break a tooth if she gritted her teeth any harder.

"*Four.*"

Somewhere in the back of her head, she could hear everyone chanting, "You're doing great! Keep pushing!" But she couldn't respond, not when every ounce of her focus was on getting this baby out of her.

"*Five!*"

The last thing she expected to hear next was a loud wail. For a moment, she thought it was coming from her own mouth. After all, she'd never in her life been through anything that difficult.

But then she realized…it was their daughter. A little girl with lungs she wasn't afraid to use.

"She's absolutely perfect," the nurse said after she did a quick newborn health check, counted fingers and toes, then swaddled the baby in a small white blanket with blue and red stripes down the side.

Full to the brim with more joy than she'd ever known was possible, Lori reached out. "Please, let me hold her." The moment the nurse laid the baby on her chest, her little girl started rooting around for her first meal. When Lori bared her breast, the baby easily latched on, drinking with a rapturous look on her pretty face.

"She's beautiful, Lori. Just like her mother." Grayson looked both joyous and overwhelmed. "Looking at the two of you—I'm falling in love all over again."

He reached out to stroke over their baby's hand, and when she curled her tiny finger around his, Lori's throat grew tight.

"I want to have a dozen more just like her," she

whispered, the pain already forgotten.

Almost forgotten, she thought as she shifted her hips slightly and winced.

The doctor cleared his throat, and Lori looked up in surprise. With her entire world centered around her daughter and husband, she'd forgotten there was anyone else in the room. From the look on his face, Grayson seemed just as surprised by the interruption.

"Lori, Grayson—congratulations. Your daughter is absolutely lovely. And Lori, if you don't mind me asking, are you an athlete, by any chance?"

"I'm a dancer."

"Ah, that explains why you are so strong. You barely needed a full five seconds of pushing. I must say, you've convinced me that my wife is right when she says ballroom dancing classes will do my health some good. In any case," he said, looking down at her chart, "you should heal up nicely. Your chart says the baby is thirty-seven weeks, but she's a perfectly healthy seven pounds and already seems to be nursing without trouble. The nurse will be back soon to take her for a little wash. If you have any questions or concerns over the next week, here is my card with my contact information." He set it on a nearby console table that was stocked with diapers and more blankets. "Don't hesitate to call, day or night. I'm very pleased that I was able to be here with both of you today." He shook their hands, then left the room, closing the door behind him.

"Can you believe we *made* her?" Lori moved the baby to her other breast. "Isn't she *amazing*?"

"I've never known anything more amazing." Grayson carefully sat on the edge of the bed so that he could be close to both of them, stroking the baby's cheek as Lori nursed her.

Lori kissed her daughter's forehead. "Now, about a name." When he groaned, she held up her hand to forestall his protests. "I know you're not the world's hugest fan of the names that I come up with for our animals." Which was why they had agreed to not even discuss baby names until their daughter was born. "Although you've got to admit that Carmelo is a pretty inspired choice for our new puppy."

"Was that just today?" He ran a hand through his hair. "It feels like a lifetime ago."

"Crazy, right? When we woke up today, little miss was still in my belly. And now here she is, loud and proud and perfect." The baby had fallen asleep nursing, so Lori lifted her into Grayson's arms.

He looked nervous for a moment, at least until he was cradling their daughter. Lori swore he was already the best dad in the whole wide world as he softly whispered, "I'll never let anyone or anything hurt you."

Witnessing the love overflow from his heart straight to their little girl made Lori choke up again.

Suddenly, he went still, his eyes meeting Lori's. "Mary. Her name should be Mary."

Finally, Lori's tears spilled over. Shifting the baby slightly to one side, he leaned down to kiss them away. All this time that they hadn't been able to decide on a name, it was because they'd been overlooking the only one that would ever have been right. Of course they should honor the woman who meant everything to Lori, her seven siblings—and everyone else who was lucky enough to be loved by Mary Sullivan.

"Mary is the *perfect* name for our baby."

CHAPTER NINE

A few minutes later, the nurse came to take little Mary for a bath, promising to have her back in fifteen minutes. Grayson was torn—he didn't want to let either the baby or Lori out of his sight. Not because he was frightened that something bad might happen to them, but simply because he loved both of them so damned much.

"I'll be fine," Lori said, reading his mind. "In fact, there's no time like the present to get started on my eighty-seven family phone calls." She picked up her phone and snapped a picture of him holding Mary. "Perfect. I'll start by texting that to everyone so that they can *ooh* and *aah* over our gorgeous girl."

Eighty-seven wasn't far off the mark. There were Sullivans *everywhere*. San Francisco, Seattle, New York, Maine, London, Australia—suffice it to say that if you closed your eyes and threw a dart at a map, you were bound to find a Sullivan living there.

"Don't get into too much trouble while we're gone." He gave Lori another kiss before heading for the door.

From the nurse's expression as they headed down the hall, she was clearly wondering what kind of trouble his wife could get into while lying in a hospital bed, having just given birth. But she didn't know Lori the way he did. Fifteen minutes was easily long enough for them to return to an entire circus performing in the small hospital room—with Lori in the lead role, dancing on a high wire in stilettos.

Not that she would have time for any of that right now. Because what she didn't yet know was that her mother and sister were far closer than a phone call away.

Though Grayson had had the shock of his life when Lori's water had broken on the beach, he'd at least had the presence of mind to send a joint text to Mary and Sophie to let them know that Lori was in labor. Thirty seconds ago, he'd received a text saying that they were only minutes away.

He couldn't wait for them to meet his little girl— and for Lori's mother to know, without a doubt, how much she meant to both of them.

From the first day he'd met Mary Sullivan, she had welcomed him into her heart with open arms, treating him like another son. And he'd loved her the same way, as a second mother he was so very lucky to have.

Gazing down at his daughter, wonder moved

through him again. He wasn't sure he'd ever look at her without thinking she was a miracle. Okay, maybe one day there might be a few speed bumps to navigate when she was a mouthy teenager, which any daughter of Lori Sullivan's was sure to be. But he'd still love every last hair on her head—and would protect her to the ends of the earth and back.

At the same time, he wasn't sure he'd be getting over the trauma of Lori's labor any time soon. As soon as she had grabbed his arm in the car, he'd known the pain from her contractions must be severe. His wife was plenty melodramatic—but never over anything physical. She could sustain injuries that would fell someone twice her size.

His heart had almost stopped a few times, first in the car and then in the delivery room. Thank God he truly believed what he'd told her on the beach—that she was the most resilient person he knew. And now he understood that the same was true for himself.

Life might not always be easy and full of roses, but there was no one he'd rather spend each day with than his sparkling, crazy-making wife.

After a quick lesson from the nurse on giving Mary a bath, putting on the tiny newborn diapers, then swaddling her in a blanket so that she felt safe in her warm cocoon, Grayson and the baby headed back down the hall to the birthing room.

With perfect timing, Mary and Sophie came through the double doors into the maternity ward. "Grayson, congratulations!" Mary kissed him on the cheek, then put her hand over her heart as she looked at her new granddaughter. "Oh my, isn't she a beauty?"

Sophie immediately reached for the baby. "Please, may I hold her?" Her expression was full of love as she nuzzled her niece. "Hello, sweet girl. I'm your Aunt Sophie, and I love you."

Though Grayson knew the baby probably still couldn't see all that clearly, he swore little Mary did a double take when she looked into Sophie's eyes. As if to say, *You look like my mama, but you're not actually her.*

Her rosebud mouth had just started to scrunch up into a wail when Lori called out, "Stop gabbing in the hallway and give me back my baby!"

Mary laughed as the four of them headed toward the delivery room. "Good to know labor hasn't taken too much out of her." But as Sophie took the baby in to her mother, Mary stopped in the hallway and put her hand on Grayson's shoulder. "How was it?"

"Lori is as strong as ever. She blew me away the entire time."

Mary didn't look at all surprised. "I'm glad to hear it. And how about you, Grayson? How are you feeling?"

He'd suspected that she'd felt his past darkness

bubbling to the surface at the baby shower. Mary Sullivan wasn't attuned only to her children's feelings, she also cared deeply about each of her children by marriage.

Now, he gripped her hands and looked into her eyes, so like his wife's. "I've never been happier."

Her smile was bright and lovely. "That's wonderful news. You and Lori are going to be wonderful parents."

"Mom!" Lori called out again, clearly impatient. "Get in here—Grayson and I have something to tell you."

Sophie's eyes were already shining when Grayson and Mary walked up to the bed. Obviously, Lori had already told her twin the baby's name.

"Honey, your daughter is so beautiful!" Mary kissed and hugged Lori. "I'm so proud of you both."

"I know. She's totally awesome, isn't she?"

Soon, the baby was cradled in Mary's arms. "Aren't you precious?"

The depth of emotion in Mary's whisper brought tears to Grayson's eyes. And he clearly wasn't the only one, because Lori sounded choked up as she said, "Mary Sullivan, meet Mary Sullivan-Tyler."

Mary looked up, stunned. "You...you named her..."

"After you." Tears spilled down Lori's cheeks as

she reached for both her mother and daughter. "I owe you everything, Mom. And I can't wait for my daughter to realize she has the coolest grannie in the entire world."

The women were all hugging and crying, and Grayson's own cheeks were wet as he stepped into the happy circle of women. His daughter was so lucky to have all of them.

As lucky as he'd felt from the start, knowing the Sullivan clan would always have his back—just as he would always have theirs.

★ ★ ★

All her life, Lori had sworn she wasn't a crier.

Only to cry while visiting with her sister and mother in the hospital—and also during every one of the bazillion phone calls she made to the bazillion members of her family around the world.

How could she be anything but totally blissed out when she had the most wonderful, incredible husband and daughter in the world?

Lori had just woken up from a short nap—giving birth *really* took it out of you—to find Grayson standing by the window, cradling little Mary in his arms. He was humming an out-of-tune, utterly unrecognizable song, and their daughter was looking up at him as though he was responsible for the sun, the moon, *and* the stars. Which, Lori could confirm, he absolutely was.

Lori's breath caught in her throat as he started to move, spinning their daughter in a slow circle, then lifting her high before lowering her into a slow, sweet dip.

Watching their first father-daughter dance, Lori fell in love all over again.

And knew that she was going to keep falling for the rest of her life.

★ ★ ★ ★ ★

For news on upcoming books, sign up for Bella Andre's New Release Newsletter:

BellaAndre.com/Newsletter

ABOUT THE AUTHOR

Having sold more than 8 million books, Bella Andre's novels have been #1 bestsellers around the world and have appeared on the *New York Times* and *USA Today* bestseller lists 84 times. She has been the #1 Ranked Author on a top 10 list that included Nora Roberts, JK Rowling, James Patterson and Steven King, and Publishers Weekly named Oak Press (the publishing company she created to publish her own books) the Fastest-Growing Independent Publisher in the US. After signing a groundbreaking 7-figure print-only deal with Harlequin MIRA, Bella's "The Sullivans" series has been released in paperback in the US, Canada, and Australia.

Known for "sensual, empowered stories enveloped in heady romance" (Publishers Weekly), her books have been Cosmopolitan Magazine "Red Hot Reads" twice and have been translated into ten languages. Winner of the Award of Excellence, The Washington Post called her "One of the top writers in America" and she has been featured by Entertainment Weekly, NPR, USA Today, Forbes, The Wall Street Journal, and TIME Magazine. A graduate of Stanford University, she has given keynote speeches at publishing conferences from Copenhagen to Berlin to San Francisco, including a standing-room-only keynote at Book Expo

America in New York City.

Bella also writes the *New York Times* bestselling "Four Weddings and a Fiasco" series as Lucy Kevin. Her sweet contemporary romances also include the USA Today bestselling Walker Island series written as Lucy Kevin.

If not behind her computer, you can find her reading her favorite authors, hiking, swimming or laughing. Married with two children, Bella splits her time between the Northern California wine country, a 100 year old log cabin in the Adirondacks, and a flat in London overlooking the Thames.

For a complete listing of books, as well as excerpts and contests, and to connect with Bella:

Sign up for Bella's newsletter:
BellaAndre.com/Newsletter

Visit Bella's website at:
www.BellaAndre.com

Follow Bella on Twitter at:
twitter.com/bellaandre

Join Bella on Facebook at:
facebook.com/bellaandrefans

Follow Bella on Instagram:
instagram.com/bellaandrebooks

Made in the USA
San Bernardino, CA
24 January 2019